11/18/11

Dear Zoey,
You are <u>our</u> wish,
and our love for
you is fierce and
unconditional. You
bring us much
happiness and joy.
Happy Adoption Day!
All our love,
Mommy & Daddy
xoxo

I Wished for You
an adoption story

is dedicated to
Matthew, Liliana, Andre, Mila
and all the wishes-come-true

Library of Congress Control Number: 2007909080

Published by Sourcebooks Jabberwocky,
an imprint of Sourcebooks, Inc.

P.O. Box 4410
Naperville, IL 60567-4410
www.sourcebooks.com
ages 4 and up

Source of Production: Leo Paper Group, Heshan City,
Guangdong Province, China
Date of Production: January 2011
Run Number: 14379

Printed in China
LEO 10 9 8 7 6 5 4 3

Also available from author & illustrator
Marianne Richmond:

The Gift of an Angel
The Gift of a Memory
Hooray for You!
The Gifts of being Grand
I Love You So...
Dear Daughter
Dear Son
Dear Granddaughter
Dear Grandson
Dear Mom
My Shoes take me Where I Want to Go
Fish Kisses and Gorilla Hugs
Happy Birthday to You!
I Love You so Much...
You are my Wish come True
Big Sister
Big Brother
If I Could Keep You Little
Night Night Book

Beginner Boards for the youngest child
simply said... and *smartly said...* mini books
for all occasions.

I Wished for You

an adoption story

By Marianne Richmond

sourcebooks
jabberwocky

Mama and Barley Bear snuggled in their favorite cuddle spot.

"Mama," said Barley. "Tell me again how I'm your *wish come true.*"

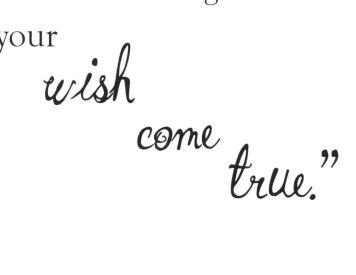

Mama smiled. Barley loved to hear

about how he was Mama's special wish.

"A long time ago," said Mama to Barley,
"a wish started growing in my heart.
At first, it was a quiet wish
that nobody knew. Then it became
an out-loud wish that grew

and *grew* and *grew.*

Until one day,
my wish
came true."

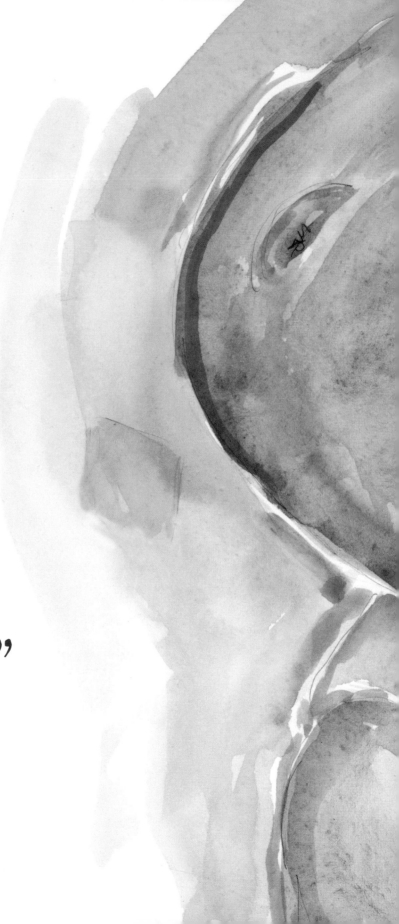

"Me!" said Barley.
"I was your
wish come true!"

"Yes," said Mama.
"You <u>are</u>
my
wish
come
true."

Barley wiggled to get more comfortable.

"*Why* did you wish
         for me, Mama?" asked Barley.

Barley wished for things like a new comic book or a
pet lizard. He had never wished for a somebody.

"Because," explained Mama, "I had
an empty place in my heart that
I wanted to fill with love
         for a special child like you.
Someone who would be
         my cuddly little one, and
I would be his Mama."

"Oh," said Barley, feeling a little unsure. He knew about how his Mama had adopted him from a far-away place.

"What about the mama who grew me in her tummy?" asked Barley. "Didn't she wish for me, too?"

Mama squeezed Barley a little tighter.

"Sometimes, Barley," said Mama, "A mama will grow a baby in her belly, and for all kinds of reasons, she'll decide she cannot be the very best mama she wants to be.

The mama who grew you loved you enough to make a different wish— a wish for a family who would love her little one with a total and adoring love.

The kind of love I have for you," said Mama.

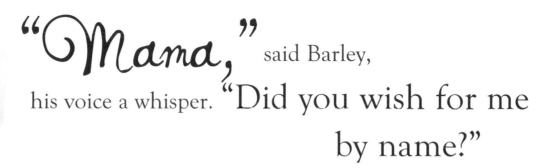

"**Mama**," said Barley, his voice a whisper. "Did you wish for me by name?"

He liked his name, he thought to himself.

Mama tilted her head to show she was remembering.

"**When** I first wished my wish," said Mama to Barley, "I didn't know your name. Or if you'd be a boy or girl. But that didn't stop my wishing. I asked God to look around and find the child who would be the perfect one for me."

Dear God, Just a reminder...

"Barley," said Mama, her eyes spilling over with tears. "Of all the children in the whole wide world, God picked you for me."

This made Barley feel really special.

There are lots of children in the world,

he reminded himself. And God picked him!

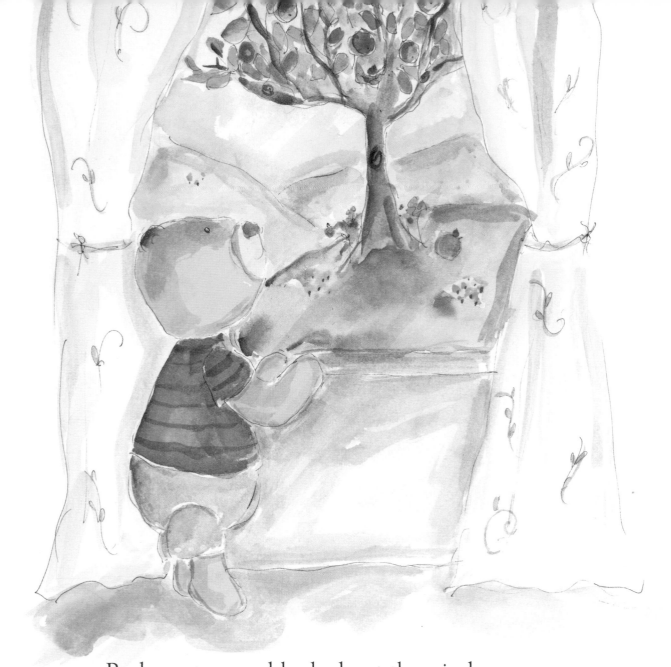

Barley got up and looked out the window

that faced the big apple tree out back.

"Did you wish for me all day, Mama?"
Barley asked. "Or only when the
stars were out?"

"**All** the time," said Mama, softly. "I wished for you with my morning coffee, and when I made my bed. I couldn't get my wish for you out from in my head."

That was a lot of wishing, thought Barley.

He thought of all the things he did at school like math and lunch and reading. He couldn't imagine wishing through all of them.

"Did you ever think," wondered Barley, "that your wish might not come true?"

"Oh yes..." said Mama, remembering how long the waiting seemed sometimes.

"I wished for you through many phone calls... and through mountains of paperwork. I wished for you while I waited and waited...

and waited.

Sometimes," said Mama, "I didn't hear any news about you for weeks or months.

But I held onto my wish tightly— like the string on a balloon."

Barley wasn't good at waiting.

He wanted his birthday to be three times a year.

"During the waiting," said Mama,
        "I would imagine *you*."

"Imagine me?" repeated Barley.

"*Yes*," said Mama.

        "I imagined what you'd look like,
or what color your fur would be.
I imagined you in your room,
        playing with your blocks and trains.
I wondered, too, if you'd like
        soccer or piano or art projects."

"Did you imagine me to look
exactly like I do?" asked Barley.

"You, Barley, are more
beautiful than
I ever dreamed,"

said Mama.

"One day..." said Mama,

brightening as she spoke,

"*One glorious,*
special,
wonderful day,
I found out my wish

was coming true."

"What did you do?" asked Barley, smiling and sitting up.

He could tell a lucky part was coming in her story.

"*I shouted for joy!*" remembered Mama, laughing.

"And I cried happy tears.

I told all my friends... and
they hugged me
and cried, too."

Barley wondered why

grown-ups

cried about

the happy stuff.

"*Everyone*," continued Mama, "knew how much I had been wishing for you!"

"**What** did you do when you first held me?" asked Barley.

As hard as he tried to remember,

he just couldn't.

He was a pretty little

Barley then.

"Oh, Barley,"
said Mama.
"I fell deeply
in love with you.
I looked into your
sweet face, and right
then, you became
my wish
come
true."

Barley felt cozy about what his Mama was telling him, but a thought niggled at him.

"Mama," said Barley. "Me and you are in the same family, but we don't look the same. You have dark fur, and I have light fur with brown ears. Is this okay?"

Mama had waited for this question.

"*Yes,* Barley, it's okay," she said. "Some families look alike, and others don't.

All families are different.

What makes a family is their *love* for each other."

That makes sense, thought Barley.

He liked Mama's answer.

He loved being part of her family.

"click"

"Do wishes *always* come true?"
asked Barley, thinking again

about the pet lizard he still wished for.

"No," said Mama. "Not all of our
wishes come true. But
don't ever stop
wishing for the hopes of
your heart."

"I won't," said Barley.

Maybe he'd ask for a goldfish instead.

"But *I* came true," said Barley, proudly.

"Yes, you did, Barley," said Mama.
"I wished for you, and you
are always and forever
my *wish*
come
true."

Mama and Barley stayed right there

in their cuddle spot, both thinking that

always and forever was a good amount of time.

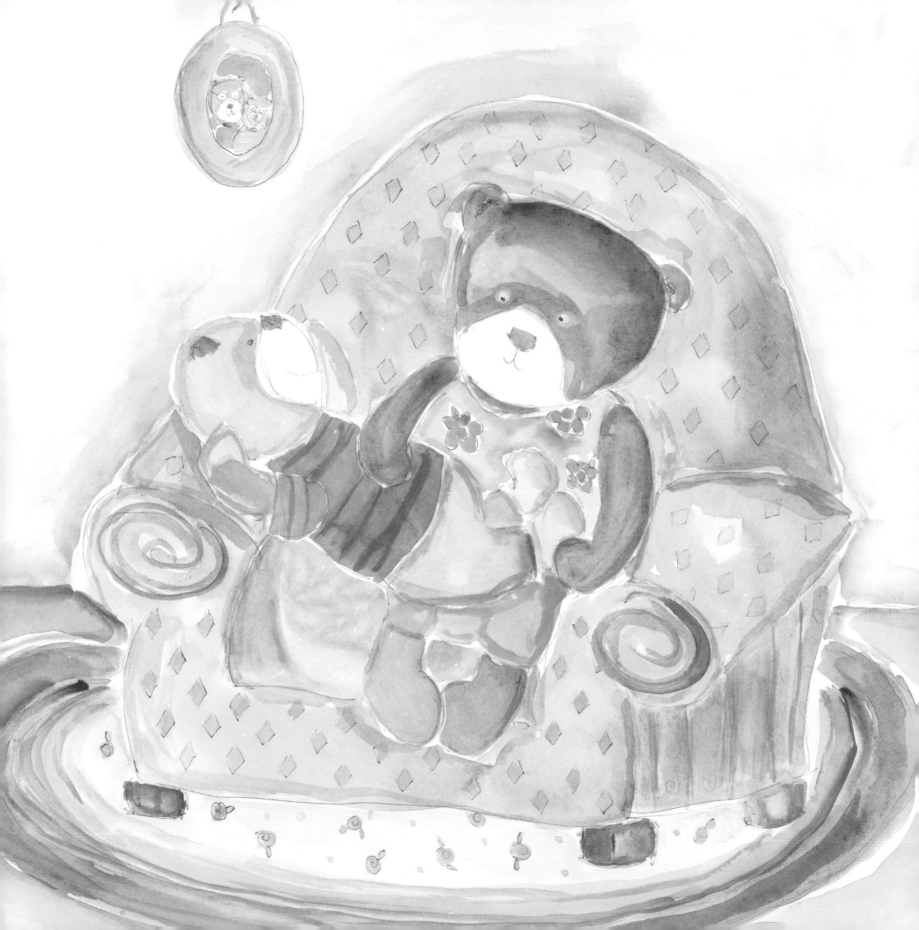

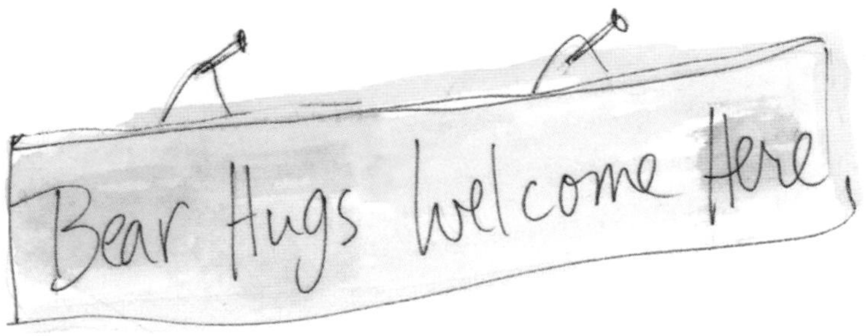
Bear Hugs Welcome Here!